Breaking His Silence

A father's journey from doubt to faith

Breaking His Silence

A father's journey from doubt to faith

By: Rodney Cleaves

Inspired by the New Testament Gospels:
Matt 9:18–25, Mark 5:22–43, Luke 8:41–56.
And, the music of Don Francisco, specifically
"Gotta Tell Somebody"

atmosphere press

Table of Contents

"A daughter builds a house in your heart, moves in and fills it with love and warmth like you've never known."

Introduction

I'd like to introduce myself and this little book. The book is purposefully small so you can read it in one or two gulps. Try to digest Parts One and Two before reading Part Three in one short sitting. What you're holding is a small piece of my ministry.

It's not only theatre, but more. Actually, it can be considered to be two books. Parts One and Two are a story about how a doubting man might have come to faith. It's a story I hope you enjoy.

Part Three is a bit of my style of ministry. It's a serious attempt to show people how theatre can be used to teach and move people.

Sometimes theatrical performance can be just entertainment, but when best used, theatre informs us, educates us, and gives us outlets to express ourselves in intimate ways we would never do as ourselves.

I've always felt more at home on stage than any other public forum. I trained for engineering and computer science, then to become a minister, then back to school for history. My interests lie in ancient Jewish and early

Christian histories and how they diverge, converge, overlap, and intertwine. The pulpit as it is currently defined is not for me.

The outlet I found to combine my faith and acting is, what I've dubbed, "Performance Preaching." I take on the persona of a biblical character and develop a socially and historically accurate back story (as nearly as I can) and for a short time become that character. I have a stable of five characters I can present in a church setting.

This book is about a man called Jairus. Three of the Gospel texts share this story. His daughter died from an illness and Jesus resurrected her. This is a well-known story, so there are no spoiler alerts here.

Jairus was my first successful biblical-based character. Part Three of this revised edition is essentially my thirty-minute presentation of "The Day Jairus Broke His Silence." It has only been updated to reflect the fictional storyline in Part One.

I recall one time when I was presenting the Jairus character to a congregation in Everett, Massachusetts. The local Pastor presented me as I had asked and I was "on." From then on I was both preacher and actor. This particular Sunday is memorable for two reasons.

One reason is that I broke my walking stick when I entered to started my presentation. That stick cost me fifty dollars at a local Renaissance Fair. I can live with that. The other memory will never leave me (this following memory skips ahead to Part Three for a moment):

About the time I was talking about Jairus' love for his daughter, a woman slid out of her seat and crouched in the middle of the church's aisle and started taking pictures of the presentation. Of course I was flattered, thinking two things: she wanted pictures of my presentation and/or she wanted pictures of my wife's fabulous costume design. I knew this lady; she was not really a friend but a close acquaintance. We attended the same seminary.

She knelt in the center aisle and raised her camera to her eyes and started snapping away. I guessed she must have taken about a dozen snapshots. Frankly, I thought this was overkill for pictures of a simple preacher.

When the services had completed, we had a chance to talk. I was floored by her confession that she was using her camera to hide her face from me. She had been crying and didn't want to anyone to see. I had no idea that what I was saying might be so powerfully received.

That one moment changed the way I viewed my own ministry. I was doing what I loved to do and it seemed to be making a difference. Over the course of my local ministry I presented my five characters many times, always to heartfelt praise from the congregation or audience. This booklet is a means to expand the message and hopefully outlive the messenger.

Literary advisors tell us, "Write what you know." Jairus' struggle was my struggle. In this second edition, I've added the journey Jairus might have taken to become the man he would be twenty years after his miracle. Part One is his journey from doubt to faith.

The story assumes Jairus' faith waxed and waned after he saw "his" miracle. Like many new converts, he was not taught and had no fellowship with other believers. Five years after his daughter's healing, we can assume Jairus' faith was wavering.

This story is biblical-based fiction. Some people (more and more these days) might say the Bible is fiction. I disagree. In my opinion the heart of this story is the Gospel truth. I try to add some richness and texture to the Bible's abbreviated story.

Performance Preaching:
A Short Tutorial

The reader will find Part Three is a different kind of story. The Performance Preacher does not *act* like a preacher; we are performing a character who *is* preaching and has a message to deliver.

Here are some simple guidelines that would seem prudent for the Performance Preacher. A few, for example, might be:

- Never act as Jesus himself unless you plan to use His exact words from the Bible translation you use.
- Stay gender and age appropriate. It would be silly for a sixty-five-year-old man to play Mary Magdalene.
- Don't make up any character's name that isn't already in the Bible. Fictitious characters should have culturally appropriate names.
- The story must not alter the gospels or their message.
- Remain historically correct.
- And, keep in mind, a bathrobe is not a costume.

Developing a backstory for a person we know so little

about is not problematic. In fact, the less the Bible tells us, the more liberties we can take, just be careful to keep true to the scriptures and the historical culture. In the case of this book, the Bible is silent about Jairus except that he was a synagogue official with a wife, a daughter, and a servant.

The gospel writers referred to Jairus as both a synagogue ruler and an official. We can assume that he was an accomplished man, a proud man, perhaps even to the point of arrogance.

When I present 'Jairus...' Part Three is what I present. I ask the worship leader to read Luke's account, then introduce me. I'll enter dressed in street clothes with my stick and a bag containing the costume my wife made. Then I start by explaining what performance preaching is and what to expect. Then, with my back toward the congregation, I dress for the part. The costume is arranged in the bag to be easy to slip on with one simple action. When the headdress, from the bottom of the bag, goes on, I am Jairus.

To create your character, read past the lines; the Bible is rich in unseen wisdom. If you understand the places and time of the writers, you can place the stories in their proper context. Build the story; then place yourself in the story.

What you're about to read may not be what really happened, but it is possible and the story doesn't alter any truths the Bible has to teach us. Quite the opposite—this story enriches the understanding of the reader.

Part One

About Three to Five Years
Post-Crucifixion

The stream was crystal clear. *This is always the best time of year*, he thought.

The runoff from the mountains brings the freshest water. He could see to the bottom through the still chilly water. Looking like he was counting every pebble, he was mesmerized by the ripples on the water. He even spied a few fish.

It was getting warmer and the wilderness was coming alive again. *Every year*, he thought, *the seasons come and go. Without fail, the wilderness lives and dies, and lives again.*

Jairus sat quietly along the bank with his seventeen-year-old daughter. She was a short distance away, wading in the water. She had just found the perfect skipping stone but hesitated. Something was moving in the bushes a few feet to her right. The stone went in her pouch as she moved slowly to the bushes.

He watched her slow, graceful, almost gliding movement to the stream's bank and the growth of nature hanging just over the water. The vegetation was a combination of acacia and thistles. One was aromatic and pleasing, the other had thorns that could tear skin apart. With her hands and a small stick she carefully parted the shrubbery and began to giggle. A small lamb had taken refuge in the bushes. It looked like it was only a few weeks old and was trembling with fear but couldn't move. It obviously tried to get away but couldn't.

That's when she noticed one of the hind hooves was caught in the thick undergrowth, right where the thistles were densest. The poor lamb was not only caught but was being impaled with every movement.

With the loving care of a professional gardener and animal handler, she bent back a few branches and eased the rear leg away from its trap. As expected, the little animal bleated and ran off to find its mother.

Jairus had to smile when he saw the lamb escape from the underbrush opposite his daughter and run away. Then his daughter's eyes met his and she brightened, sharing loving smiles a hundred feet apart. She giggled a little and he smiled.

Another pleasant memory made, another story to tell and the feeling of helping another of God's creatures and seeing his daughter's contented face.

Then, a wave of emotion came over him like a cold night air. He, his daughter, and his wife were fast becoming outcasts in their own village. It had been five years since she was cured of her sickness. Was it a cure, or a resurrection like it had seemed to be at the time? It was so long ago. Maybe she was just sleeping and the rabbi woke her when he touched her. So much time had passed he was unsure. For a long time now, he had been wrestling with doubt. He was gazing at the far side of the stream, not focusing on anything.

In that long-ago night, he had been filled with so much excitement and gratitude for her recovery that he would have believed anything. He remembered the woman with a bleeding issue. Had she been cured? It certainly seemed so. Was his servant mistaken when he came running to tell Jairus his daughter had died? Over the years his emotions ran the gamut, from fear because of her sickness to elation when she arose from her bed. Now, to confusion and doubt, not even sure what he had seen with his own eyes. At forty-seven years he thought he should have his religious faith settled. He'd been searching for meaning since his daughter's illness.

Many of his friends and neighbors have been saying that nothing remarkable ever actually happened. Some had gone so far as to say Jairus made it all up just to gain sympathy for his family. He supposed it was for not having a son. He only had the one daughter; no more children would be coming to his family. And, while he loved his daughter very much, he did ache for a son. Did he really witness a miracle, or was it just the way events played out?

He had remained quiet, like he was told. The people in Capernaum knew his daughter had been ill, then over night she was fine. Rumors were rampant, but he never said a word. He couldn't defend himself, nor explain the events of that night. He kept quiet and let the rumors fester. Even his precious daughter did not know what happened that night. She was ill, then she was well. What else did she need to know?

His daughter finally skipped that rock across the stream. Four hops, good for her! It was practically a record. She was already searching for another good skipping stone.

His mind continued to wander. It's been, what, three years now since Jesus was crucified? His followers say He walked out of that grave and ascended to Heaven. Their detractors say the body was stolen or he didn't die at all. Whom to believe? Jairus had so many questions, so much confusion. The priests in Jerusalem, and the rabbis in his own synagogue, work hard to dispel any notion that Jesus was anything more than an itinerant preacher.

All that turmoil over one man. But, there's his daughter, happy and healthy only feet away. For her first few years, he was proud to have a baby daughter, then she got older. As she became a young woman she started spending more time with her mother, and Jairus began to feel left out but he knew that wasn't true. He didn't like sharing her with anyone. He found refuge in his position at the synagogue and his Jewish faith.

This is now, that was then. Back then it couldn't be denied, after Jesus left that night she was healthy again after weeks of illness. Then, she became his little girl again. In reality, the bond that grew after that night encompassed the whole family. All three of them, including his servant, were like one bonded soul. It was hard to explain, but everything changed that night.

Maybe that's part of his answer. After his encounter with Jesus, their lives were changed. Maybe it is time to go talk to a few of The Master's followers again.

"Peter might be nearby, maybe even James," he thought out loud.

"Who are Peter and James?" his daughter asked as she approached him.

Jairus was so lost in thought he didn't see her approach. He had never said anything to his daughter about that night.

How does one tell a child she died and was brought back to life? This thought came easy to him. He had to consciously remember he had doubts. She had never died, so she could not have been brought back to life, right? He simply didn't know anymore.

She continued, "Did you see that lamb I freed from the bushes?" she was giggling. "It was so cute and gentle. It was afraid of me at first but the second I released its leg from the branches, it stepped out, and stopped and turned to look at me as if to thank me. Then it ran away. It's a shame we have to sacrifice such adorable little animals during Passover."

Jairus started to give her a lesson about sacrifices and why a sacrifice would mean nothing if you didn't care about the animal. Then he stopped himself before he could speak. An odd thought passed through him.

He was again lost in thought as he and his daughter started for home. Thinking to himself, ... *if a sacrifice is supposed to be a personal animal that you care for, what is the sacrificial value in purchasing a couple of doves at the Temple then handing them over to the priest a few minutes later? It is no sacrifice to slaughter two doves you just bought, you have no attachment.*

It's like Cain's sacrifice was not acceptable before God. He couldn't have had an attachment to a bowl of vegetables.

This idea hit like nothing before. He had never considered this and never heard anyone else talk about it. It was as if he was the first person to ever ponder such a thing. Questions, answers, and more questions consumed his thoughts.

However, he had consolation that clarity was on its way. He had already decided what to do next. He needed to find answers as soon as he could. He already knew what his friends and the priests would say. It's time to hear the other point of view.

Roads to Answers

Jairus knew Peter's mother-in-law had lived in Capernaum but their paths rarely crossed. Peter had originally grown up in Bethsaida and he had heard Peter might be back there. A trip to Bethsaida would be much shorter than going all the way to Jerusalem.

The trip to Bethsaida would take less than two hours. It was just on the other side of the northern Galilean shore and a little inland. If Peter, or another follower, was not there, he would have to go back through Capernaum to get to Jerusalem, anyway. Then, Jerusalem would be a full two-day or more journey.

Jairus arrived in Bethsaida midmorning. There were more people than he had remembered since his last visit. This is where Jesus fed the 5,000, or so he had been told. Peter, Andrew, and Philip all came from this village or nearby. *I'll start in the market square,* he thought to himself.

He made his way to the market and started asking for the three men's names to anyone who would talk to him. When no one knew or remembered them, he asked if anyone remembered the rabbi, Jesus. All shook their head 'no' and he continued further into the city. He continued asking strangers along the road. He decided he could give himself one more hour before returning home. If he rushed he could get back to Capernaum before sunset.

One man remembered Peter but hadn't seen him in years. He also remembered hearing about Jesus and thought He might be a great prophet.

"It's too bad the Romans killed him. I guess he was too controversial for them," the stranger said.

Jairus asked, "Might you have any idea where Peter, Andrew, or Philip are now?"

"As far as I know," the man said, "the whole lot of them are in the Holy City stirring up trouble. Their misguided rabbi is dead, so I'm not sure what kind of trouble they can cause. They are an odd bunch, you would do well to stay away."

And then, the man was gone, obviously not wanting to talk anymore.

Jairus headed back to his home. He had to get some provisions and a good night's rest before starting for Jerusalem in the morning.

When he returned to Capernaum, he spoke with no one, not even his wife. He was deep in thought, troubling thought. For five years he had struggled to come to terms between what he learned to believe as a young man and what he witnessed in his own home. The rumors he heard around the village were unsettling.

His thoughts turned to the beautiful mosaic on his synagogue's floor. He was trying to put his thoughts together like that mosaic. He had some pieces but not enough. He just couldn't see the whole picture, at least not yet. He needed to find his answers, but even now he wasn't sure what the questions were. He was empty with doubt.

The next morning he arose early, well before first light, and prepared to pack his donkey. But the donkey and his provision were nowhere in sight. He searched several neighbors' yards, assuming the animal had wandered off as it was prone to do now and then.

Just around the corner, he spotted his donkey being led by his servant. The donkey's back had more provisions than he wanted. He hadn't planned on taking a tent, a lean-to would suffice, and there was no need for so much food and so many changes of clothes.

"I needed to go buy more food," said his servant. "You only packed enough for one. You didn't think I was going to let you travel to Jerusalem by yourself, did you? It's at least a two-day walk each way and there is no telling how long you'll be staying," he continued.

Jairus knew better than to argue. This man was an employee, but when he spoke like this he was not to be ignored.

"Let me say good-bye to my family, then we will be off,"

said Jairus who was resigned to having company on his journey. He had been looking forward to the solitude.

The household was awake and alive, so he said a quick good-bye to his wife and daughter and took his leave.

The road to Jerusalem was largely one long walking path due south. They would skirt the West side of the Sea of Galilee for about a half a day. Then about a half day later sleep under the stars, or maybe their tent. Water could be scarce. Jairus was glad his servant packed several wineskins. One wineskin for water and the rest for wine. On the second day they would start early and with luck be in Jerusalem by nightfall.

They walked in near silence for about an hour when the servant asked, "What if asking for these men raises suspicion?"

"What of it," said Jairus. "We are just trying to find a few old friends."

The servant went on, "That's the problem, the Temple authorities are hunting and dispersing all the Jesus followers they can find. I heard the Temple Priests were hiring men to lead the persecutions so they could appear impartial. Apparently they are Roman citizens, so it appears Rome is behind the effort to harass all of the followers.

"Your daughter told me why you want to go to Jerusalem. She said you were questioning your very soul and you seek answers about the Messiah."

Jairus said, "Yes, ever since that man healed her, everything I've learned all my life has been thrown into chaos. I'm not even sure whether she was healed or resurrected. Maybe He was just showing off for the crowd.

The servant caught this last thought and replied, "What crowd? Only you and your wife were in the room and you told me the man said to tell no one. You only told me, because we are close. The crowd outside had no knowledge of what happened. I still don't know where the mourners came from," he said, chuckling.

Nothing was said for quite some time when Jairus asked, "Did you follow Jesus 'ministry after he left Capernaum? I tried but couldn't because of my synagogue duties. I heard a few things here and there, but not much."

The servant paused and thought about what to say for a little bit. "Yes, there was something about Him I could not deny. I saw lives being changed, not only your daughter's life. Do you remember that pesky woman He helped? You told me you were there. Have you seen her?"

Jairus shook his head 'no.' Frankly, after that day, he had given her little thought.

The servant continued, "Well, she has a husband now, and a child of her own. They live in a small house outside of Capernaum. I think he's a farmer."

"So, did Jesus really heal her or was it a coincidence and she would be fine today anyway?" Jairus said aloud but almost to himself.

The servant said, "As far as I'm concerned, it was Jesus. They called Him Master, remember?"

They made small talk but mostly continued the trip in silence. That night they stayed outdoors off the side of the road with a small group of others making the same journey. While they were among the group resting and waiting for daylight, Jairus asked a few of the men if anyone knew of Jesus, Peter, James, or any others associated with Jesus. No one could help and a few men seemed annoyed to be asked.

After a few minutes, one of the men approached Jairus and took him aside and asked him if he was a follower.

"No," said Jairus. "I did meet Him once and I knew a few of His followers. I just want to find them and ask a few questions. I hear rumors and I overhear people talking about events surrounding Jesus and I want to know why. Who was the man? Why does He still seem to have such a hold on His followers?"

The stranger studied him for a moment and took Jairus further away from the camp and in a low voice said, "Be very careful whom you talk to and how you approach them. You could get yourself in trouble. Draw this sign in the dirt and be quick to brush it away if anyone suspicious or the authorities get too close."

The man then used the toe of his sandal and drew two small arcs in the dirt. The arcs intersected at one end and overlapped on the other end. It was a vague outline of a fish.

"Ask if they know the fisherman," he said. "If they look confused or angry erase it and move on. If you have found someone who can help you, they'll either brush out the fish you drew or draw another with their toe. Let that man lead you to a safe place and you can ask your questions. Take care to brush the symbol aside before you walk away. We need to keep this symbol as secret as possible."

The next morning Jairus and his servant continued to Jerusalem hoping to be there by nightfall and find lodging. They walked the entire day with little conversation. Both were wondering how they would find the people they were to identify. Then, what to do if they found them.

As they neared the city they realized there were fewer crowds than usual compared to their previous visits. It occurred to both of them they usually came to Jerusalem during Passover and other Holy Events. Today, Jerusalem was fairly quiet by comparison.

Since it was approaching sunset, they looked for lodging. They found a small inn to accommodate them with a stable off to the side. The animal was tied up, the remaining provisions were carried to their small room, and they rested.

Jerusalem

Both Jairus and his servant had a fair knowledge of the streets of Jerusalem after so many visits. However, neither had ever lived in the Holy City. The morning of their first day they arose early, ate from their provisions and left to roam the city.

Before splitting up to shorten their search, they decided to walk to the Temple together. Perhaps luck would show itself, but in reality, they both wanted to see the Temple without the countless people who gather on the High Holy Days. The Temple was a short walk from their lodging and they arrived in no time.

They passed through the Gentiles' Courtyard and ascended the steps, purposely built uneven to force the pilgrim to contemplate their destination. They reached the platform, which encircled the entire Temple, and faced the Gate Beautiful. The gate was barred from the inside. Neither had ever known this gate to be locked, but today was not a High Holy Day, so there was no need for it to remain open.

The General Entrance Gate was around the corner to their left. This gate was open and after a short wait, they entered the Outer, or Women's, Court. This area was a common gathering place for Jews from all sects. If they were to find anyone of interest it would either be here or in the Gentiles' Court just outside.

They wandered around the court to take in the sights and see whether anyone looked familiar. Jairus drew a fish in the sand on the floor, but no one paid any attention to it. He erased it and tried again at the other end of the court. Same result.

They decided to try the Gentiles' Court, but this time left through the Music Gate on the opposite side of the Outer Court.

As soon as they stepped outside they saw knots of people discussing everything worth discussing: religion, politics, Roman occupation, farming, fishing, and general neighborly gossip. The Temple was the center of Jerusalem life. No one, though, was talking about Jesus or his followers. Jairus went one way and the servant went the other way.

A few feet down the side wall the servant stopped and drew a fish in the sand. Some people saw it and ignored it, but most people kept to themselves and walked past him. Meanwhile, Jairus tried the same thing.

After a little time, they had lost sight of each other. Jairus was drawing fish on the ground and waiting for someone to notice, like a vendor selling fresh fruit.

His servant was watching faces, looking for anyone with a calm countenance, or anyone he might know. He thought there must be a way about someone he could recognize. This didn't work for him either.

It had been a wasted morning so both men started back to meet at the inn by the agreed hour. Jairus arrived first.

There was a man near the inn's doorway and he was watching Jairus with suspicion. Jairus noticed him but was unconcerned. The street was jammed with people of all types and Jairus felt safe with a crowd nearby.

When Jairus was about ten feet away from the inn's door the man approached, raised his hand, and stopped him.

"Please come with me, I need to talk to you," the man said.

The man led Jairus around a street corner for a private conversation. Now Jairus was worried. He had no idea who this man was.

"What do you think you are doing showing the fisherman's mark all over the Temple grounds? Do you have any idea who could see it and get the wrong impression?" He said without anger, fairly calm, but determined to make a point.

Jairus said, "I'm seeking old friends and was told that sign would lead me to them."

"Ask me, maybe I can help, I know a few people," the man

said.

Jairus went on, "About five years ago I met three men named Peter, James, and John. They came to my house with their teacher." He was still afraid to speak Jesus ' name because he didn't know this man in front of him.

"I might know these men. Was their teacher named Jesus? Did all four of them visit your home?" the man asked.

"Their teacher's name was Jesus, yes. I understand the Romans killed him about three years ago. I want to ask a few questions, that's all. Just questions."

Before the man could speak, Jairus 'servant arrived and spotted them. He approached the two of them.

"Master," his servant said, "I had no success this morning."

"Is this man with you?" the man asked Jairus.

Jairus said, "Yes, he was also there that night. He has been a loyal employee for nearly twenty years. We came here together to find these men or someone who believes like them."

The man took a deep breath and let it out slowly as if pondering what to do next. For some reason, this put Jairus and his servant at ease.

"I know the three men you seek, and several others. John

will be nearby later today. Tell me why you want to meet him and I'll ask if he can see you."

Jairus was nervous again; this was his one chance. If he said the wrong thing this man might not take him to see John.

He said, "I think Jesus healed my daughter that night when they all visited my home. I want to talk to someone about what happened and why so many people continue to be so excited about Him three years after his death. Back then I thought only a sorcerer could heal people, now I want to know more about Him."

"I understand." the man said, "I'm sure John would like to talk to you. Both of you or just you?" the man asked.

"Both," Jairus simply said.

The man then said, "Give me a little time and I'll be back." He turned and folded into the crowded street.

As they both watched him walk away, the servant said, "I guess we will get those answers after all. Now, I wonder if we have the questions."

Jairus clucked, "We have some time to talk about it. Let's go eat."

They repaired to their shared room to eat and discuss their next step. After finishing the last of their food they decided to wait for the man outside in the street and try to formulate what to ask.

Jairus said, "We need to ask why these men stayed with Jesus all that time. What was His draw? These men left their homes and wandered around with Him for His entire ministry. Was it worth it?"

The servant responded with, "In that same thought, why did they continue the rabbi's work? Why not just go home and back to fishing or whatever they did?"

"Good point. What keeps these men proclaiming a message so much against the Temple teachings?"

"And, I heard there were other healings besides your daughter, how did he do that? I don't think he was a physician or sorcerer."

Jairus said, "All he did was touch her. And, not just healings, didn't you tell me you heard rumors about Him changing water into wine? And, cast out demons?"

"Yes, I heard that story from a traveler passing through Capernaum a long time ago. Jesus 'ministry has a lot of people talking about his message. Some like what he taught, others do not."

Jairus replied, "Apparently these men thought Jesus ' teachings were exactly what we needed to hear. If anything, His followers seem more fervent now than ever before. We hear about oppressions and maybe even death but these men all seem to stay with what their teacher taught. I wonder how many believers are here?"

"True," the servant said, "I wish he would get here soon.

"I just remembered that someone said His body was never seen after His death. Some even say he walked out of the grave."

Jairus replied, "Maybe his followers stole it to prove a point."

"All good ideas and questions to ask. Maybe when we are introduced, we should tell him we have doubts, then let him talk. We might not have to ask anything at all, he might explain everything to us."

They continued to wait. As the shadows started getting longer, they saw a familiar figure walking toward them.

"Come with me, this way," the man said. "John is waiting for you. He remembers the day he, with Jesus, Peter, and James, were all at your house. He even remembers your daughter."

They did not have to walk far. Only four or five streets away there was a small house with a walled off courtyard. The man led them into the courtyard through a side gateway. After entering, he turned and barred the door.

John wasn't exactly waiting for them. He was talking to a small gaggle of men. He was animated and waving his arms all over. He was talking fast and was obviously excited. The men listening to him were enraptured and hung on every word.

The three of them stood off a short distance, not wanting to intrude. The courtyard was small so they felt conspicuous. After a short time, John acknowledged them with a nod and told his small audience that he had other duties to attend, and asked whether they could return later. The group of men departed.

John beckoned them over and invited the three men to sit.

"My friend here tells me you seek answers. Answers to questions you are not even sure how to ask. Let me start by welcoming you to my home. In a minute we will have something to eat and drink while we talk.

"Jairus, I remember you and the night we came to your home. I remember watching Jesus raise your daughter from the dead. Jesus, Peter, my brother James, and I all talked about that night several times. You were truly blessed with a great miracle. But now you struggle because you can't believe your own eyes?" he asked, hoping for a response.

Jairus 'servant jumped in, "Did He really heal that woman in the street just before coming to our house, too?"

John was quick to answer, "Her faith healed her. She knew deep in her heart of hearts that Jesus could have healed her but she couldn't get to Him. It was a big crowd, remember? I think when she touched His robe she was trying to get his attention. Her faith is what got Jesus ' attention. When he consented to heal her, she was instantly cured.

"She was a citizen in your own village. You had known her for years and many physicians tried and failed to find a cure for her. She met Jesus and she was healed, simple as that.

"You didn't come all this way to ask about her. You want to know about us and why we persevere with Jesus ' pronouncements long after his supposed death."

Jairus couldn't keep quiet. "Supposed death? The Romans are very good at killing Jews. He was crucified, right? If he was crucified, he was killed. He's dead!"

John had heard it before, "Yes, I suppose he was dead for a few days, but then he arose back to life. Not only life as we know it but more glorious. I saw Him, I talked to Him just hours after his resurrection. I know He's still alive.

"On that day, many of us were in a house not far from here. He told us not to touch him because He had not yet ascended to the Father. He was clearly alive and standing there, right in front of us, but He was different, too. There was an obvious light about him, and the scent of perfume as if He had been prepared for burial. But He wasn't buried."

Jairus spoke, "So all your faith in Him hinges on His resurrection?"

"Yes, and no," said John, "His resurrection proved beyond all doubt He was truly the Son of God. If He could defeat death He could do anything. If He could do anything, then all the deeds we witnessed were real and divinely blessed. His entire message, all he said, was true. It had to be true, God doesn't lie. We realized we had been with the Messiah all that time."

Jairus replied, intoning, "But what keeps you going all this time, so long after his death? It seems you have more faith now than you did before His crucifixion."

Jairus 'servant stayed silent still but was aching to get into the conversation.

John said, "Yes, all of us have a much more powerful faith now and it grows every day. We build each other up. We pray directly to Jesus and always draw strength from prayer. Did you hear what happened on the fiftieth day?"

Both Jairus and his servant shook their heads 'no.'

John continued, "The twelve of us had gathered for a meeting. We had several hundred new converts from many nations with us that day, and out of nowhere we were visited by a thunderous noise and hot wind, like fire it almost consumed us. And within a few seconds, we were all speaking in different languages!

"We were speaking the languages of the people in the crowd. They could all hear the Lord's message in their own language. All the people there, converts and soon-to-be converts alike, heard the same message in their own tongue. No one needed a translator to understand what they heard. A miracle!

"Jesus had promised to send us aid and that hot wind was the Holy Spirit, sent by our Lord to help us stay strong in our faith. After the gathering, we retired to our meeting room to compare our experiences. We all realized we had become filled with new Spirit, a sense of real purpose, and a boldness none of us had ever felt before.

"I'll tell you something a little personal. After Jesus's resurrection, we were scared to death. For weeks, we were afraid to answer a knock at the door for fear of being arrested or worse. They had killed our Lord and His body was missing. We had seen him, but the authorities had not. We were afraid to say too much out loud. We had faith, but no heart.

"We tried to talk to as many people as would listen. The word was being spread, but slowly. After the Feast of Pentecost, we didn't care what happened to us. The Word of the Lord had to be preached, the good news must be circulated fast and wide. All He told us and all we saw and must be true. All our doubt disappeared."

The servant jumped in, "But, you are facing oppression and persecution every day. Wouldn't it be easier to just be quiet and go back to fishing? Someday one of you will be killed."

John said, "That has already happened. Not long ago a man strong in his faith named Stephen was stoned to death by an angry crowd right here in Jerusalem. I witnessed it, but was helpless to stop it. Just before he died I saw Stephen's face light up and heard him shout that he saw Heaven open up and saw Jesus standing at the right hand of God.

"He was gone a few moments later. Think of all the things he could have uttered as his last words, but instead, he exclaimed he was looking at God and Jesus. As for me, that was not just faith, it was fact."

Hours passed and Jairus and his servant continued to listen to John and get all their questions answered. John talked mostly about his personal travels with Jesus and the miracles he saw. Sometimes, the conversation heated up and sometimes the three men had a good laugh.

The day was long gone and the streets were almost too dark to navigate. After a few wrong turns, Jairus and his servant found their inn. John had invited them to remain in Jerusalem for a few days to talk to others and perhaps attend a meeting of the burgeoning church.

When they settled into their room Jairus said, "That was an interesting visit and he answered most of my questions. But I'm sorry to say it was just words to me. I understood everything he said and even agree with him. A good question would be 'where's the body,' and he answered that.

"However, there's no denying he and his friends had a life-changing experience. They saw the resurrected Jesus, they received the gift of speaking in other languages. He knows about all this from his soul. He was excited when he talked about his time with Jesus.

"How do we get that same assurance?"

His servant said, "I was wondering the same thing. These men's lives were changed, and they became new men. How do we become new men, if we even want that at all?"

Jairus said, "Well, John did say Jesus taught belief in Him and his Word was the only way to God. He didn't say anything about living a pious life, or a life changing experience, just faith. That goes against everything I was led to believe all my life. I was taught that only through obedience to the Law of Moses can we find God.

"I've always tried to follow the Law but, to be honest, have come up short most of the time. But the only way to see God is to follow the Law, right? Isn't that everyone's goal?

"We will stay a while longer and attend a meeting or two."

They drifted off to sleep, each one lost in his own thoughts, pondering the day and wondering what tomorrow would bring. John told them to come back mid-afternoon and someone would take them to the meeting place. Until then, they should enjoy the city and take in what it has to offer.

Questions and Doubts

The next morning, they arose at their usual time and prepared themselves for the day.

Jairus said, "We will go to the market to purchase supplies for the journey home and maybe find small gifts for my family."

Then they were off to see what they could find for the home journey. They bought new wineskins, wine, bread, dried fruits, and other essentials. Jairus found a new knife for himself and some fine cloth and trinkets for his wife. His servant bought nothing.

They returned to the inn to store their purchases and relax for the midday meal. Soon after, they started wandering the streets looking for John's house. Loitering in Jerusalem, waiting for a gathering to take place somewhere at a time unknown, seemed fruitless.

The way to John's house had seemed easy enough the day before, but not today. Both Jairus and his servant thought they remembered how to find John's house but after a little while, they were hopelessly lost. They were walking together, more like friends than master and servant. They wandered aimlessly for a couple of hours with no luck finding any place familiar.

Jairus spotted the sign first: a small, perfectly square ashlar with the symbol of a fish carved into it. They had passed this house earlier, but this was the first time they noticed the sign. The stone was not part of the wall. It was freestanding on top of the wall. It was obvious the small stone could be moved and carried from place to place to show where meetings were being held.

With more than just a little trepidation, they approached the door and knocked. Maybe we should just walk in? The servant tried again looking at Jairus as if to say, *Why not? Maybe they'll come eventually if we knock hard enough.*

After a short while, someone did come to the door. Jairus did not recognize the man, nor did the man recognize Jairus, but the man did see that Jairus and his servant seemed to pose no threat. The door opened and the man asked who they were and why they were there.

"We are friends of John. We were invited," spoke Jairus.

The man said his name was Matthias and they should enter and wait. There were many more people expected. Matthias was the man elected to replace Judas before the miracle on the Feast of Pentecost, after Jesus 'crucifixion.

Matthias said, "We are informal here. Sit anywhere. I am not sure who will be speaking today, perhaps more than one person. It won't be too long. Is there anything I can help you with?"

"We had a conversation with John yesterday. He told us a lot about Jesus and you men; he told us about the miracles and His message and He answered all our questions. He even told us about Jesus 'beatings and His crucifixion.

"But, I fear we have more questions now than we did before talking with John. That's why we came today."

"What questions? Perhaps I can help. We have a little time."

Jairus hesitated for a moment. He still wasn't sure about this man or even if they were in the right place. What if this were a Roman trap? Yesterday, John had warned them about speaking too freely to strangers. But, there was the fisherman's sign at the door. He asked the most personal question he could imagine.

"How do we get what you have? I mean, you seem different from most Jews, but you have also abandoned the teachings of Moses."

Matthias looked them right in the eye and said, "We have not abandoned Moses, not at all. We are completing the law of Moses. The law hasn't been forgotten; Jesus said He came to fulfill the law, not destroy it. He taught us that the Pharisees had perverted the law for their own selfish purposes. All of scripture was written to point to Jesus.

"We were looking for a Messiah to free us from Rome.

When you think about it, Rome is just here for a time. The afterlife is for eternity and Jesus came to give us a direct path to God Himself and to be with Him and the Father forever, starting now.

"The scripture supports everything Jesus said and Jesus showed us the way for all of us, both Jew and Gentile, to communicate with God and be with Him and the Father forever."

Jairus said, "You are the third person who told us Jesus came to complete the Law. I don't understand what that means. How do you complete a law?"

Matthias thought about his answer for a moment, then said, "When you close a service in the synagogue, you've completed that service. That service is put away, but the lesson is not forgotten. The next service will have a new message. Jesus completed our bondage to the law, and has given us a new way to reach God."

Jairus took it all in and realized John had said the same thing but with different words. Somehow Matthias made it sound easier.

Matthias continued, "And, yes we are different. Those of us who follow Jesus have come to realize how the Pharisees have twisted the teachings of Moses. Jesus called them vipers, and hypocrites. Did you know that?"

"I had no idea Jesus spoke out again the Temple Priests. Is that why they had the Roman's kill him?"

Matthias answered, "It appears so, He was challenging their authority and comfortable living. He didn't just speak poorly of them, He hated the whole religious system. He said religion should serve men, not control them. This didn't make sense to us. Jesus was not concerned with religion, He was concerned with men's relationship to God. He also spoke often about helping the less fortunate. Have you ever heard a Temple Priest tell you to give to the poor, or care for the widows and orphans? It all starts with a true heart for God, not the Temple."

Jairus interrupted, "I am beginning to understand better now. How do I get what you have? You say you're a Jesus follower but He's dead. How do you follow a dead man?"

"He *is* alive, didn't John tell you? He's alive and with the Father right now. We speak to Him in prayer and He speaks to us in our hearts. We don't hear His voice, but when you are a true believer, you know when He speaks to you. It's no fantasy."

Jairus said, "John talked quite a long time about the day Jesus rose from the dead, its proof, and his travels with Jesus, but it's still hard to believe."

"And you are still having a hard time believing it?" Matthias asked.

"If I could reconcile my mind with the truth of His resurrection, it would be easier to believe."

Matthias smiled and said, "Then, ask yourself this, 'where is the body?'

"Where?"

"We know, but I'll leave that for you to ponder. We will be hearing from someone soon."

John, who had been there all along, stood in the middle of the gathering. There were about twenty men in the small room; all became silent and listened to every word John had to say.

He could swear there was a glow about John. Not so much a glow, but when John spoke, he had such authority there was no denying he was passionate about his time with Jesus.

John was telling the truth, as he knew it, and his conviction was obvious. Jairus didn't hear anything new. John and Matthias had said it all to him and his servant. Jairus noticed that his servant had eased himself through the crowd to get closer to John.

Jairus was in the process of thinking, *These are still just words to me, what do these people have that I don't?* When he heard John say, "Let us all pray."

John said a prayer completely unlike anything Jairus had ever heard in the synagogue. He was offering reverence to God and Jesus both, and then he seemed to just start talking to Jesus like he was standing right next to him. He called Him "Lord." Then John invited the men to each pray their own prayer if they wished.

John told them, "If you're unsure what to pray, here is how Jesus taught us to pray: praise the Father and His name, pray for the kingdom to come, and do His bidding, ask for our daily sustenance, ask for forgiveness and to help you to forgive others, to keep us away from evil situations, to keep us away from the evil one, and to pray in His name.

"Just have a conversation with God. Sometimes you will hear Him right away and sometimes the answer comes later."

Jairus thought, *That last thing John said must have been for my sake, my answer will come later. We were never taught to pray like that. How does one talk to God? We're not even allowed to say his name.*

He sat off to the side silently watching.

A few men drifted out, a few stayed and waited to talk to John. Jairus was thinking he wanted to talk to John too, but he still had no idea what to say or ask. It seemed all his questions had been answered, but he couldn't think of anything else he needed to know. All he had were empty doubts.

He did see his servant talking with a small group of men.

One of the men leaving brushed by Jairus, "I don't think I have ever seen you here before. Are you new?"

Jairus nodded 'yes.' "My friend and I are just visiting. We plan to return to Capernaum in the morning. I manage the synagogue there."

"This must all be strange and new to you. You have been part of the system for so long, I wonder if what John said makes any sense to you at all."

Jairus said, "You understand my confusion. I hear the words and most of it makes sense, but it's just not believable. How can a man talk to God? How can Jesus, risen or not, promise eternal existence with the Father?"

"Well, think of it this way. Jesus was either truly the Son of God or completely delusional. It all turns on whether you believe He was raised from the dead or not. If you believe He did, he's the Son of God. If you believe He did not, he was an insane fool, and we're fools for following Him. No one in this room is planning to upend his life for a myth.

"My name is Asher. You and your man must come to my home to sup. We can talk over my wife's delicious meal and then I can take you back to where you are staying. I live a few minutes' walk from here. Everything in Jerusalem is close, right?" He clapped Jairus on the shoulder like an old friend.

"Yes, we can come, thank you. Wait here a minute while I get my companion."

Jairus walked toward the knot of men and retrieved his servant, saying, "We are going to that man's home for supper," pointing at Asher, "are you finished here?"

"Yes," said the servant, "It's been quite a day. It all makes sense to me now. Let's go."

"This is Asher," Jairus said as the three men left the house.

As they exited, Jairus noticed the ashlar with the fisherman's symbol was gone from the top of the wall. He guessed the last person to arrive probably took it down and it would soon be used at another location.

Asher

Asher lived in the Lower Section about a street's distance away from the southern wall. Jairus had no idea where they had been. They had stumbled onto the meeting house, therefore for all he knew, they could have been anywhere in the city. Asher led them through winding streets so confusing that Jairus could never find his way back.

There was no outside enclosure. Once inside the door, Jairus could see two rooms and a brick-and-clay stairway to a one-room upper level. The entire house could fit comfortably in Jairus 'courtyard back in Capernaum. Asher led them up the stairs through the back to a rooftop sitting area. Jairus realized they were directly over one of the two rooms he saw below.

The sitting area was small but comfortable. The night air was warm with a light breeze. Asher left for a moment to find his wife and let her know they had company. He found her in what turned out to be a courtyard after all. This place was in the back of the house. She would prepare fish, fruits, bread, olive oil, and wine for the guests.

Asher returned to his guests and took a seat. "A little food will be here shortly. Tell me about Capernaum and your journey to the Holy City. You said you were here for answers, but I suspect there is more to the story. Answers you can get anywhere, even in Capernaum. You traveled a fair distance for a lot more than answers, my friends."

His servant looked at Jairus as if to ask, *Can I speak first?* "Something changed in me today, but I'd like to know more," he said to Asher.

"Tell me," said Asher

Jairus was intent on what the man had to say as well.

The servant started talking, "I listened to every word John had to say. It all made sense, all the details, all the little facts seemed to come together as one big story. When I combined the pieces I was hearing, along with John's obvious passion, I started to really believe what he was saying. It wasn't like the effect strong wine brings; it was a down-in-my-stomach knowledge that what I was hearing was just as real as seeing a newborn baby.

"John said I should be baptized, and I would receive the help of the Holy Spirit."

Asher nodded his agreement, "Yes, that, and you need to find other believers as well. We hold each other up by attending house meetings and praying together. It sounds like you have trusted the Lord. I can arrange to get you baptized and then we can..."

Asher's wife arrived with the meal, "Please eat and enjoy."

Asher continued, "First, we thank God for this meal. We do this because we know nothing comes without His help.

"Later, if you wish, I can introduce you to other believers. Before he was beheaded, John the baptizer used to baptize people in the River Jordan. Since you are leaving for Capernaum tomorrow, that's too far to go today."

Asher led the men in prayer for the food that was prepared by his wife. As they started to eat and drink, Asher looked at Jairus and asked, "You still have questions? Perhaps I can answer a few for you."

Jairus started, "As I said back at the meeting, all I hear are words, I understand them, some make sense, but what John is teaching is against everything I was taught to believe. I am in charge of the synagogue in Capernaum. Sometimes I even lead the services. How can I turn my back on everything holy to me?"

Asher spoke first. "Remember when I said Jesus came to complete the law of Moses? Embracing Jesus has nothing to do with ignoring your faith—it is just the opposite. Jesus said He fulfilled the Law. You know what that means? Because of Him, the Law is finished, we are all under a different covenant with God now. We are no longer bound to the Law and worried about how to live within it. Now, we focus on Jesus. He loves us so much that He sacrificed Himself on the Roman cross so that we all can be with the Father."

Jairus almost pounced, saying, "I've heard the thing about completing the Law, but you are saying He Sacrificed himself? The Romans killed Him. You are not saying He willingly went to His crucifixion, are you?"

"Of course He did," said Asher. "Consider all the miracles He performed, not to mention His actual resurrection. Anyway, Jesus could have avoided His last trip to Jerusalem or He could have been less fervent with His preaching.

"He walked to His own crucifixion to ensure all of us can have direct communion with God the Father, and to prove, once and for all, He was truly the Son of God."

Jairus asked, "So, all I need to do is believe Jesus is Lord of all, and God sent Him? I would not be turning my back on what I already hold dear?"

"Yes and no," Asher intoned. "You must believe in your heart of hearts, be baptized, and no, you don't have to turn your back on the Temple but you will begin to understand the new promise Jesus offered us.

"None of us can ever live up to all the demands of the Law, not even the High Priest himself. However, we can all believe in Jesus and trust in His sovereignty."

Jairus 'servant chimed in: "What is involved with baptism?" He was eager. "When can I be baptized?"

Asher said, "When you find a believer and running water,

ask to be baptized. He, or someone he knows, will take you into the water and fully immerse you in the water. Do this in the name of the Father, the Son, and the Holy Spirit and you will emerge as a new man."

"That's all there is to it? It sounds too easy," said the servant.

Asher said, "That's all. You have already done the hard part, you've learned a new way of thinking and come to believe."

Then he turned to Jairus. Speaking with a loving, but hard, voice, he said, "You, my new friend, have a little more to do. When you can profess your belief, you can be baptized. Right now, I think your pride is getting in the way. You are holding on to your position at the synagogue and the beliefs you grew up with."

Jairus was stunned at that but silent. This man looked right into his soul. More pondering.

The three of them continued talking for a long time. The basics of the conversation didn't change. Jairus and his servant kept asking the same questions and expecting clarifications but using different words all night. Asher was patient and was never short-tempered. He answered all their questions with grace and with the countenance of a good teacher.

The day was done, Asher led them back to the inn, said

good-bye, and offered blessings for their safe travel.

Back to Capernaum

Jairus and his servant departed the inn just as the sun was rising in the east. They knew they couldn't get to Capernaum by nightfall but they wanted to travel as far as they could on the first day. They found their way through the city to the Water Gate and onto the road pointing north to Capernaum.

The way was more crowded with people and animals going north than it was coming south a few days ago. However, the road was wide and open with plenty of room for everyone. They settled into a walking pattern and kept quiet for a few miles.

"It has been an interesting few days so far," Jairus 'servant started. "You found all your answers but they don't make sense to you. I came along to give you company and the same voices gave me my answers and made a believer of me."

Jairus answered, "I know, I think I believe but I just don't feel it inside. John said to believe in Jesus means everlasting life, whatever that means. Really, I do believe but my position at the synagogue and my family are all at risk. I have a lot to lose if I change now. You have nothing to lose.

"If I change now my wife, will think I have lost my mind. My daughter will never understand and reject me. If you change now, you can start a family with a woman who agrees with you."

Jairus thought to himself, *If the truth would be told, I don't want to believe. There is too much at stake.*

His servant took a serious tone. "I'll help you. Keep it quiet at first. When you have enough faith and understanding to stand on your own, you tell them. By then they will already see a change in you, they'll know something is happening. You have been paying me to assist you and your family for a long time. I won't leave you now.

"I don't know where this will take me either. As I learn, I'll teach. Still, I would like to find someone who has been a believer for a while so I can be baptized."

Maybe we will get lucky when we get home, Jairus mumbled almost to himself. His gaze was down like he was studying the road and he was deep in thought. He remained pensive for quite some time.

During the northward journey Jairus began to study the families and faces of the families on the road. Some were miserable and hated being on the road. Some families had joy in their hearts just because they were families on an adventure.

He said, "I wish my daughter was with us right now. I want to put my right arm around her, like that man ahead of us. I miss her. His daughter must be, what, five or six years old? My daughter would be embarrassed if I showed that much affection."

"I was wondering when you would bring her into the conversation. It's been at least three days since you mentioned her. I don't think you've gone so long being this silent about her."

They continued in silence for a while, all the time Jairus' mind was only on his daughter. He had never ached to see her this much. She was now his focus, not John or any of the other men he met in the last few days.

Around the eleventh hour, as the day began to close, they started looking for a place to camp. They found a good spot just a little southeast of the village of Belvoir, west of the River Jordan.

They found themselves in a wilderness grove on the edge of a small section of land surrounding the communal water well. They had shelter, fresh water, and time to reflect.

Since they were a distance off the main road, there were only a few other travelers nearby. Many were locals who came for the cool, clean water. At one campsite in the clearing that night was a family he saw on the road.

Jairus reflected to himself, *That man seems to have the*

same affection for his daughter as I do for mine. I'm not alone. He can get away with it. As an official at the synagogue, I cannot. What would people say?

Open affection was frowned upon by the Temple authorities and that attitude filtered down to the local synagogues. Jairus struggled to observe the Law but nothing made sense when it came to his daughter. If his daughter had been a son, his love would be sanctioned, but for a daughter, he was supposed to stay away and let his wife handle the intimacies. He remembered the scene of his daughter a few days ago near the stream.

A tiny seed had been planted.

Jairus 'servant wandered to the well and drew the fisherman's mark in the dirt. Then, stood back.

Jairus said, "We're not supposed to do that. Remember, we were told?"

"I want to see who notices it. I'll stand back and watch. There's no danger. No one here knows us."

Jairus turned and walked into the thicker trees off to the side of the clearing in search of solitude. He needed to think in silence. Solitude was a welcome destination for his filled mind.

As he left, he turned and said, "Set up the tent and start a fire, maybe somewhere over there." He gestured with his outstretched arm. "Wherever you can be close enough to watch the well to see who notices your sign," he almost snorted on the word 'sign.' Then, Jairus turned away and walked into the woods.

Nothing was in his focus now except his whirring thoughts. His eyes could not focus on the tiniest of leaves, let alone the entire grove in front of him. His footing was uncertain as he stumbled forward.

Jairus walked and thought, almost mumbling to himself, "Dear God, what do I do now? I've seen the truth but how do I turn my back on a lifetime of education and tradition? And my family, they will think I've gone insane. The rabbis will think I've lost my mind and shun me."

He raised his face to the heavens. "Are You really up there, watching us? How do I know what to do? I believe You are the Lord, but do You really see me? Dear God, I want to be happy, I want to do what is right.

"But what's right?"

He was getting fidgety. Needing to move, he walked on. The well was off to his side in the clearing, but Jairus stayed out of sight. While he wandered the grove and wondered about his future he noticed a stout stick off in the bushes. The stick was straight, came up to about his chin, and big enough around to clasp comfortably in one hand. Somehow, the stick found its way into his possession.

He kept the stick; it gave him something to do with his

hands. He picked at the bark and small growths to occupy his mind.

Daughter, wife, Jesus, John, Matthias, many men and women, and his own manservant. All of them were speaking to me, not shouting at me tonight, just trying to reason with me. What did it all mean? Jairus was thinking.

His thoughts were as thick and elusive as flies on a carcass. Not one thought was his and his alone, they flew in and out of his head.

He continued to walk well past sunset thinking the same thoughts over and over again. He believed but he didn't believe, he wanted a better life for his family but didn't want to embarrass them. *How was all that possible?*

While Jairus was off thinking about his future, his servant was preparing the meal. The evening prayer was upon him, but he was sure Jairus would be back soon, so he waited.

The fire was settling into comfortable coals and he warmed himself to stave off the chill. They had no meat to cook. He waited and kept his eye on the well.

Around the first hour of the night a man came to the well and walked around as if searching. Then he stopped and looked at the ground. He swept away the servant's sign and moved a few feet away and drew another sign in the dirt with his right foot. The servant could tell, even from a distance, it was the fisherman's sign. The man looked around and walked away.

The servant got up and walked to the well to make sure he was right. The sign was where he expected it. He rubbed it away with his foot and looked around for the man. He was standing about fifty feet away staring straight at him. They started walking toward each other. As they approached, the stranger asked, "Do you know the fisherman?"

The servant said, "Yes, I just learned of Him in the Holy City. I need answers and a little help."

"Call me Taavi," the stranger said. "We can sit here and talk."

The servant gave Taavi his name and started talking about their visit with the men in Jerusalem. He told Taavi he already believed but was hoping that a real baptism in running water would help make things clearer for him.

"We can baptize you tomorrow if you like. The Jordan River is only a few minutes' walk east from here. However, baptism only completes your belief; it is not the cause of your belief."

"'Cause' and 'completes,' I keep hearing those words. What does that mean?"

Taavi continued, "When Jesus left us He gave us His last command. He told us to go into all the world, preaching His Word, and baptizing in the name of the Father, the

Son, and Holy Spirit.

"You've listened to people preaching to you. I think you believe, that's the cause. Now, we can baptize you, and you will have taken the next step, that's the completion. Well, actually, almost the completion. Baptism is more like an outward declaration of your acceptance of the new word. Think of it as a marriage, only you're marrying an idea, or spirit.

The servant had to ponder this for a while and said, "When he returns, I'll talk to my master about staying another day. Can we meet on the morrow and go to the river?"

"I saw your tent across the clearing. Wait for me there and I'll find you after morning prayer. I live nearby. If your master can't let you go or doesn't want to join us, nothing will be lost. I'm sure there are many people in Capernaum who can help you."

"Are you saying there are many Jesus believers in Capernaum?" Out of the corner of his eye he noticed Jairus crossing the clearing toward their tent. "I know of a few believers but rarely talk to them."

"That is okay," Taavi said, "I'll explain more tomorrow. You'll be fine. Tend to your employer now and have a good night's sleep, and I'll see you shortly after daybreak."

"Wait," the servant said, "I have a few more questions." They talked a little longer.

Jairus returned to the tent site and found it empty. He knew his servant was nearby, so wasn't worried. The tent was prepared and the fire was warm. He went to the donkey and found his new knife. He retrieved it from his pack.

Finding a place to sit near the fire, he started debarking and shaping his new walking stick. The bark and wood scraps found their way to the flames. He watched the sparks fly as he carved the stick. He hadn't had so much fun in days. He was beginning to relax.

He was getting pretty good at aiming straight into the fire. Every well-aimed sliver sparked and burned like a firefly. He was laughing out loud and had no idea why.

His servant came into the campsite and sat with Jairus in the glow of the fire. "I would like to change our plans for tomorrow. Can we stay another day? I found a nearby believer who can baptize me in the Jordan tomorrow morning."

Jairus responded, "I understand you are eager to do this thing, but Capernaum awaits and I want to return soon. I am sure someone in Capernaum can baptize you anytime you are ready."

His servant pleaded, "Perhaps, yes, I know. But, I feel the need to be baptized as soon as possible. Please, I have been a loyal servant, I have never asked for anything for myself.

"We could strike the tent as soon as we arise and take

everything with us to the river, then leave for Capernaum directly after my baptism. We will only be delayed a few hours and I'm sure, if we push, we can get to Capernaum tomorrow night. We made good progress today."

Jairus continued quietly carving the new walking stick. For the moment the joy had left him. He couldn't get the slivers to the embers. He was done with the bark and was now shaping the ends. He was so lost in thought, he didn't see that he was carving deeper into the stick than he should. A lot more than bark was finding its way to, and around, the fire.

He said, "Did you prepare any food for tonight?"

Jairus was completely ignoring his servant's plea for a small detour.

"Yes, I have some fruit to go with bread and oil. We have wine, then some food. We have four new wineskins, three with wine and one with water. Can you spread the blanket? I'll fetch it."

Jairus set aside his knife and stick and spread the blanket and found two stone cups for the wine, but did little else.

His servant returned with one wineskin and poured wine for both of them. Then he brought the food and sat down with Jairus. Fruit, nuts, bread and oil, and wine—a decent meal for two men away from home.

"Sir," the servant started, "I know I'm only an employee,

but we've been together since before your daughter was born. Do you remember that night?

"It was the first time we got drunk together, too many toasts to your new son before you even had a child. It's true, only friends get drunk together, not a master and his servant.

"I will never forget your disappointment when 'your son ' turned out to be a daughter. You almost spat in the poor baby's face, remember?"

They both stifled a melancholy snort. *Yes, he certainly did remember that night, a short seventeen years ago. It should be a happy memory, but tonight it was just a distant memory. Why wasn't his daughter on the road with him now? Her absence hurt more than it should. Now? When did these feeling become so strong?*

Jairus started laughing. "And you! Once you held her for the first time, I couldn't tear her away from you. You loved that little girl as much I did. I know you love her still."

He got serious, "I always thought you stayed with us all this time because of her. When she was sick you took care of her as much as her mother did."

The servant sighed. "Jairus," it now seemed appropriate, for the first time, to use his master's name, "I love your whole family, including you. This is why I think of you as a friend and why I accompanied you on this journey. I stay because you are the only real family I have. This man,

Taavi, might be my way to some kind of salvation."

"I know," was all he could say.

Jairus was completely unfazed. He got his aim back and was hitting the fire with every stroke of his blade.

"Master, in my mind you are my friend, my most treasured friend. I came to Jerusalem with you because I knew we were both seeking the same answers."

Jairus, looking off in the distance, said, "Tomorrow, when Taavi arrives, we'll be ready and see what we can do. If we go to the river, well, we go the river. We can leave for Capernaum from there."

Neither said another word. They ate what they had in silence and watched the coals begin to fade.

Jairus' servant broke the reverie. "Thank you. I'll clean up now and pack as much as I can so the morning will be easier."

Jairus stayed where he was, lost in thought and continuing to shape his new stick. His servant stored and packed what he could and lay down to sleep. Having completed his new walking stick, he lay down much later. His walking stick, with a curiously narrow end, was close by his side.

The last day of their journey started slowly. They arose when it was still dark, ate breakfast, and finished packing. There were a few other travelers and families in the area all doing the same.

Jairus didn't sleep much that night. He had a sense of not having slept but was fully awake when the daylight came. He awoke and assisted his man.

Taavi arrived a few minutes after morning prayer with a little girl at his side. "What are we to do today? Are we going to the river together or are you starting your travel to Capernaum? If we go to the river, you will have a surprise waiting for you."

The girl clung to Taavi at the sight of the strangers.

Jairus spoke first. "Are you Taavi? My name is Jairus. My man spoke of you."

"Yes, last night I told him I would be here at this time. If you want to visit the River Jordan, I can take you there now. However, if you want to leave for Capernaum, I understand. As I told your man, nothing is lost, I live nearby."

"We will go to the river," Jairus said softly, looking at his feet. He turned and smiled at the girl. "Is this your daughter?"

Taavi said, "Yes, she wanted to come today. She'll be quiet and I'm sure won't bother you."

"Bother us? I'm sure she'll be a welcome addition to our little band. I have a daughter of my own," Jairus said.

He was already finding a little of his joy again. "Your daughter reminds me a little bit of my daughter about ten years ago."

Taavi indicated the direction and beckoned the two men to follow him. They exited the area to the east and found a deeply rutted road. They were walking directly into the rising sun. It was only a few minutes later that they noticed the unmistakable earthy scent of the water. They continued walking and their nostrils were full of the smells of the river.

There was a clearing just ahead and, as they got closer, they began to see the water just past the clearing. They heard a low murmur and even some laughter.

Jairus was walking behind Taavi and his servant, who was leading the donkey. The road was uneven and Jairus was glad he made this new stick. It felt good in his hand. He looked through the vegetation and saw several people in the clearing and on the shore of the river.

Some of the people he saw had joyous faces and some had serious faces. He wasn't sure what to think of the scene before him. His servant and Taavi had been talking nonstop since they left the well. His mind was empty and he was quiet. He realized he was concentrating more on the road than his destination.

Jairus had barely noticed when Taavi's daughter had fallen back and taken his hand. Many pleasant but older thoughts filled him now. *Why would she trust me with her hand? No matter, it felt loving and innocent.* A little more joy filled Jairus. He breathed deeper, more alive.

They entered the clearing with the riverbank about a hundred feet farther along. There were people, many people, at the river's edge.

Taavi leaned into Jairus 'servant and said, "Remember when I said to look for a surprise here for you? Look out there about a halfway from the shore. That is one of Jesus ' apostles. He was one of the twelve chosen to be with Jesus during His entire ministry. He recently returned from Ethiopia and wanted to come here to spread the Word and to baptize all who come to him. I have seen as many as three hundred people here in one day.

"He is Philip. Sometimes he would start baptizing at the first hour and not finish until well after sunset. This is one of his greatest joys."

His servant turned to Jairus, "Sir, Taavi and I will go to the water and prepare for the baptism. Would you take the donkey?"

"No, tie the donkey to a tree somewhere over there. Find a tree with some grass around it so the beast can graze. I'll stay here to ensure it won't run away."

Jairus watched the donkey being tied to a nearby tree then walked to the spot. He found an old tree stump nearby and sat down. From there he had an unobstructed view of the entire clearing and riverbank. He saw Philip in the water with a line of about twenty-five men snaking its way back to the bank. Another hundred or so in the clearing or on the bank either waiting to be baptized or expecting someone to exit the river.

As Taavi's daughter ran back to her father, Jairus had a poignant thought about when he and his daughter had started venturing into the woods and he tried to teach her a little about the wonders of what God had made. Watching Taavi and his daughter together made Jairus think of the best of times when he and his daughter were together.

Then, of course, her "night." Everything was for her.

His attention was drawn back to the men in the river.

The process was the same for each man. Philip was waist deep in the water. He would beckon the next man in line and ask his name. Philip would place his left hand on the man's head and raise his right hand to the sky. He would ask if the man believed in the Lord Jesus, His Word, and if he repents of his sins. He then says:

"I baptize you," the man's name, "in the name of the Father, the Son, and Holy Spirit."

He then helps the man completely submerge. After immersion, the man just pops up out of the water and walks to shore. There didn't seem to be much to it. Except for the waiting in line, the whole process took less than half a minute.

Jairus thought, *Can such a simple act, such a short ceremony, actually change a person? Philip asked each man if he believed and repented of sin, then dunks him in the water.*

Jairus continued watching in silence while Philip took one after the other as they presented themselves. He saw his good servant just entering the water. He noticed the men leaving the water. They were happy and animated. Unlike the Temple rituals where people left sullen and usually in a foul mood, these men were eager to get wet. What does getting dunked in the river mean?

Getting wet, is that all baptism really is? What is that all about? Anyone can jump in a river. What's happening here? His thoughts still weren't clear.

His servant was inching closer now.

He studied the faces of the men leaving the water. They had not changed and yet they were different. Their change seemed to be like his change the night his daughter was born. One moment he was worried, the next moment he was elated.

He thought, *Is baptism like my daughter being born?*

Jairus was hypnotized by the scene in front him. This new teaching is obviously reaching all types of people. And, he had learned that once converted, most people stayed converted. Some have even gone to their death for their new belief. Stephen came to mind.

As his servant was about three people away from Philip, Jairus was certain Philip looked right at him. Eye to eye, almost spirit to spirit, nearly a hundred feet away and Philip seemed to be speaking directly to him. The connection was momentarily unbreakable.

Then It Happened

He stood as his man came back from the river grinning from ear to ear.

"I feel wonderful, like a new man," he told Jairus. "I'm ready to return to Capernaum now. These clothes will dry while we walk."

Jairus didn't hear his servant, as he was focusing on a distant point, the ringing in his ears pulsating with his heartbeat. In a trance-like state, he mumbled:

"Wait here." Jairus had been in a dream state for two full days.

He had become completely unaware of his surroundings, focusing only on Philip. It was as though he were looking through a hollow reed directly at Philip. He saw nothing else, except the good man's face.

Jairus was almost numb with anticipation. He dropped his walking stick, removed his fine cloak and headdress, and started toward the riverbank. He felt as though his feet were walking themselves. He was shuffling in the sand, yet his legs were too heavy to move with his own effort.

It's time, he thought to himself as he gathered speed. He all but ran into the water, bypassing every other man already in line. His focus was on Philip alone. The water was cold but he didn't care. *For my daughter,* he thought.

"Now! I must be baptized now! Move! Out of my way! I can't wait any longer. I must get to Philip!"

This was quite a contrast compared to the others patiently waiting. They turned his way and saw what could only be described as a mad man. He was running knee-deep then waist-deep in the water, soaking all those in line. Jairus was frantic and unable to hold his own counsel.

"I must be baptized now! I believe, I believe in what Jesus taught!" He didn't realize he was shouting, almost incoherent, to all those nearby. Even his servant and Taavi could hear his shouting. They were almost amused but knew what Jairus was experiencing.

He reached Philip, who looked around pleadingly to the others waiting patiently. His eyes said, *This man needs me now; you can wait a moment longer.*

Jairus sputtered, "My name is Jairus. I'm the Synagogue Manager in Capernaum. I believe Jesus is the Messiah and came back to life for us all. I need to be baptized."

Jairus was talking so fast his words came out like one long word:

"MynameisJairusI'mtheSynagogueManagerinCapernaumI believeJesusisTheMessiahandwasraisedfromthedeadforus allIneedtobebaptized."

Philip had to smile. This was the first time anything like this had ever happened. He faced Jairus, placed his left hand on his head, raised his right hand, and said, "I baptize you, Jairus, in the name of the Father, the Son, and the Holy Spirit."

Philip helped Jairus submerge and stand up again. When Jairus emerged from the water, he shook his head and brought both hands up to clear his eyes. He took a deep breath and looked skyward.

He felt like he was seeing the sky for the first time. The sun never shined so bright. The sky was never bluer and the air never clearer or sweeter. His heart was still racing and his breathing was so rapid that he felt faint. He felt like he had just run a footrace for his life. He was giddy, but not tired. He was invigorated!

All these feelings caught him completely off guard. No one warned him this would happen. Matthias had said baptism would not be a life-changing event. This was amazing—he was happier now than the day his daughter was born. How can that be?

Jairus could not contain himself. He wrapped Philip with a hug, almost breaking the poor apostle into halves. "It's real," he said to no one in particular, but Philip could hear, "It's really real! I'm as light as a feather!"

He ran out of the water as fast as he could. Leaving the river was much easier than entering a few minutes earlier. It seemed he was almost walking above the water, like he was flying! He had to get to his servant and Taavi, who were at the water's edge and watching Jairus act like a crazed man. His answers had been settled, but now he already had more questions. They could wait, they were not important.

At forty-seven years old, Jairus felt like he had been reborn as a new man.

Part Two

Historical Context

In today's light, many readers will find some of this story a little odd. The characters in this story lived during and just after, Jesus' time. Part One might have taken place around 40 AD; Part Three (the Performance Sermon) will be taking place around 60 AD.

In this little book you never saw a reference to the Bible. There was no "Bible" in this timeframe. The Jews of Jairus' time only knew the Hebrew scriptures. Today we would call their scriptures the Old Testament. Not one letter of the New Testament had been inked in Jairus' day.

Saul, the man who would become Paul, had not yet met Jesus on the road to Damascus. In fact, he was still called Saul when Jairus was baptized. Also, in Jairus' lifetime, it is unlikely anyone had heard the term 'Christian' (see Acts 11:26). The early church in this story was trying to keep their Jewish faith intact. From the 2020 perspective, we'd say that the Jesus followers were trying to form a new Jewish offshoot, not a whole new religion.

However, with today's hindsight, we know that a new religion was inevitable. Jesus and His followers were in the midst of overturning (or expanding on, elucidating, reteaching, reformulating, and reexplaining) everything they had grown up with in the Jewish tradition. And worse, they threatened the comfortable position of the Temple authorities.

The Temple officials had a good living in the money-changing business. They could impose Temple taxes on a whim, not to mention the hefty, unregulated pay they gave themselves. Their specialty was Jewish population control.

Over time, we know the Temple hierarchy did not have to worry about the new believers. Rome was more than eager to carry out all oppression until 312 AD, when Constantine became the first Christian Roman Emperor. Some will say it was in name only, but at least Constantine accepted the new Christian sect.

We know from the historical record that the new church during these two hundred eighty years, before Constantine, must have had a horrible time. At least a dozen generations of believers lived, worshipped, and died without ever knowing peace. But even during all this oppression and persecution the church flourished.

It is arguably estimated by the time Constantine declared Rome to be a Christian nation, about ten percent of all Roman citizens had converted to Christianity. The First Council of Nicaea in 325 AD formalized the fledgling church and started us toward what we have today.

Unfortunately, after Constantine died in Constantinople in 337 AD, the new emperor resumed Roman paganism, and

Christian oppression and persecution started anew.

Jairus didn't live through all this turmoil. During his time the Christians were certainly oppressed, but mostly they were misunderstood, mistrusted, and mostly shunned by the population.

We can be certain Jairus had an uphill battle. The story you read surmised that he either resigned his synagogue position or was fired. His friends and neighbors in Capernaum marginalized him and his family. Even though he had doubts, he persevered until he found his answers.

Part Three of this story will deal with what Jairus might have been doing when he reached his sixties. By the time Jairus started inviting people to his home he would have had many meetings and discussions with the leaders of the newly formed church. And, he attended many house church services for his own training and spiritual growth. It's unlikely there were too many dedicated church buildings during Jairus' lifetime. Most archeological scholars believe dedicated church buildings weren't built until the mid-third century.

Like today, there were hardcore believers, holiday believers, cultural believers, and believers that ran hot and cold. This story was written with the idea that Jairus was one of the hardcore. He would have learned as much as he could about Jesus and his mission here before he left this earth.

It is conceivable Jairus could have become an expert on

Jesus and His earthly mission. And even more conceivable, he would have shared that knowledge. Once Jairus came to terms with his own unbelief and his daughter's miracle he would have been, as we say today, "on fire for Christ."

This book started out, and indeed the first version called *Jairus Breaks His Silence*, as a way for this author to share his "Performance Preaching" ministry. Today, my ministry is closed and I'm enjoying retirement, photography, art, and writing. My wife, also retired, is a carpenter. She's rebuilding our house from basement to roof.

A few times you read a reference to the hour of the day, the first hour, the sixth hour, and so on. In those days an hour was not as rigid as today. People in that era considered a day broken in two twelve-hour sections each. The day's twelve hours started at sunup, the first hour. The sixth hour was when the sun was highest, and the twelfth hour was when the sun set. Then, they'd start again with the first hour of the evening.

In Part Three, the performance sermon, you will see Jairus notices his audience was composed of "Greeks and Romans"; this was the Jewish common terminology at the time, used to describe people from foreign lands. There might have been people from any nation, but the Jews of that era would have called them either "Greeks" or "Romans."

I hope this story has given you some idea of what the earliest believers might have endured.

Let's leave you with one last little historical tidbit. Simcha Jacobovici, an archeological journalist, may have found evidence of the High Priest Caiaphas coming to believe in Jesus. The Israeli Antiquities Authority believes it has found the High Priest's house. A remote control robotic camera was sent in and videoed what appeared to be spikes. Possibly used in a crucifixion.

Why would Caiaphas keep such things, if it's even his house? Obviously, there's no way to know for sure if they were from Jesus' crucifixion, or any crucifixion at all. Maybe the man collected spikes. It's all conjecture and we're likely to never really know. But, that's what makes archeology and history so much fun.

A Little Theology to Chew On

In Jairus' time the Jewish concepts of heaven and hell were quite different from the modern day Christian view. Jairus would have been under a belief system that defined heaven as a return to the Garden of Eden, and hell as an amorphous dark pit.

The Jewish belief in death is unlike anything modern Christians believe. The dead "sleep" until the resurrection. On the resurrection day, the evil will be sent to hell, the righteous will be with God in a Garden of Eden setting.

Hell even has a different name. In Hebrew it's called Sheol. Sheol has another name you might recognize, Hades. Defining piety in a person is has always been difficult for Jew and Christian alike.

In today's Christian theology, piety has no place in heaven or hell. Only trust in the Messiah makes a person heaven bound. Hell is so called because it's complete separation from God.

Although, it is still unlike the Christian point of view, most of the West's concept of hell comes from a classic work called *The Divine Comedy* by Dante Alighieri. The reader might recognize the common name, Dante's *Inferno*, which is actually about one-third of the total poem. Dante's *Inferno* is not scriptural.

The Christian belief, based on the Epistles and the Book of Revelation, is that heaven and hell are respectively abject paradise and eternal death. We've all heard phrases like "lake of fire," "Judgment Day," "book of life," and a few more. Jairus never would have never heard those phrases. He would have familiarity with metaphors like "paradise," "the throne of God," "great chasm," and maybe "the pit."

The New Testament writers made it clear that the oppressors of the Jewish Nation were the Romans. And, along with Roman oppression, the Temple authorities were complicit in keeping the local population under control and off balance.

Between the years 38 to 41 AD, most Christians had been expelled from Rome. Many returned to Jerusalem and stirred up a revolt against Rome. The oppression under Roman rule continued until the year 70 when Rome destroyed the Temple in retribution. And by then, the Christians were establishing enclaves throughout the region and had long broken with the Jewish faith.

This story presupposes Jairus to be a few years older than Jesus. It's fair to assume that Jairus' ministry would have long been closed by the time the second temple fell. More than likely, by then, he had left this earth.

I hope that Jesus, his wife, daughter, and Levi were in his

last thoughts. If so, he died a contented man.

Part Three

The Preaching Performance

You've now read a story about what could have happened to Jairus after his daughter's miracle. What follows is the actual sermon this author would deliver as a performance sermon. It's no different from an actor portraying a real person. It's not meticulously memorized like a script but, rather, a deeply held story. A full understanding of the character allows the preacher to deliver his "one man," or hopefully "one woman" show/sermon with conviction.

I've delivered this sermon as Jairus all over the Greater Boston area. Depending on the circumstances, the performance could take anywhere from ten minutes to nearly forty minutes. If you want to develop your own Performance Preaching Character, do the following: write the script, learn as much as you can about the character and the history, and practice like crazy.

If you know the character and the message, you can improvise on the spot. Sometimes, I even take questions. As you can see from Part One, it's not just the Biblical character everyone knows. What the Bible tell us is a snapshot in time of the character. It's up to you to make the character come completely alive.

When I visit a new church and begin to prepare for the service, I ask the officiant to read one of the Gospel accounts. Luke's version (Luke 8:41–56) from the New American Standard Bible reads:

> And there came a man named Jairus, and he was an official of the synagogue; and he fell at Jesus' feet, and began to implore Him to come to his house; for he had an only daughter, about twelve years old, and she was dying. But as He went, the crowds were pressing against Him.
>
> And a woman who had a hemorrhage for twelve years, and could not be healed by anyone, came up behind Him and touched the fringe of His cloak, and immediately her hemorrhage stopped.
>
> And Jesus said, "Who is the one who touched Me?" And while they were all denying it, Peter said, "Master, the people are crowding and pressing in on You."
>
> But Jesus said, "Someone did touch Me, for I was aware that power had gone out of Me."
>
> When the woman saw that she had not escaped notice, she came trembling and fell down before Him, and declared in the presence of all the people the reason why she had touched Him, and how she had been immediately healed.
>
> And He said to her, "Daughter, your faith has made you well; go in peace."
>
> While He was still speaking, someone *came from the house of the synagogue official, saying, "Your daughter has died; do not trouble the Teacher anymore."
>
> But when Jesus heard this, He answered him, "Do not be afraid any longer; only believe, and she will be made well."
>
> When He came to the house, He did not allow anyone to enter with Him, except Peter and John and James, and the girl's father and mother.
>
> Now they were all weeping and lamenting for her; but He said, "Stop weeping, for she has not died, but is asleep."
>
> And they began laughing at Him, knowing that she had died.
>
> He, however, took her by the hand and called, saying,

"Child, arise!"
And her spirit returned, and she got up immediately; and
He gave orders for something to be given her to eat.
Her parents were amazed; but He instructed them to tell no
one what had happened.

Now, let us combine the written and the unwritten word and imagine Jairus about twenty years after his daughter's healing miracle.

On the Day Jairus Broke His Silence...

Picture a dwelling in a quiet section in Capernaum. Bigger than most, smaller than some, it was typically opulent for a well-to-do man. There was a little bit of open land but no animals in sight. This wasn't the residence of a farmer or fisherman. It was the house of an official, a pillar of the community. Well kept and tidy, it was clearly the home of a happy family.

Jairus' wife has a few things to say before we start.

"My husband is a good man, a godly man. But after all, he is a man. He never puts anything away, and I'm the one expected to know where everything is. He doesn't prepare the meals, but he knows how to eat them! And our daughter is his daughter, as if I had nothing to do with her. He'd want you to believe he bore her and I was just an observer. At least that is what he tells everyone.

"Actually, I know better. They share a special bond. Deeper than most fathers and daughters.

"I am lucky: my husband likes me and I like him. He has always treated me like a valued friend and partner. Like

"

most men, he wanted a son, but when our daughter was born, he was disappointed, for a moment. He scooped her up and loved her with a fierceness I've seen in no other man. And, I admire him. He stands proud for the things he truly believes.

"Let me tell you about something that happened to us perhaps twenty years ago when we met a man who changed my husband forever. He had a few rough years but now he obsesses about this man.

"But this isn't fair, I talk too much. This is Jairus' story . A few days ago he was getting ready to talk to people like he does almost every week and he was obviously distracted."

The story continues.

People had been arriving all morning; the street in front of his house was almost full to impassible. For nearly twenty years they had been coming to hear this former synagogue official talk about events that no one else in authority dared speak. It was common knowledge that Jairus had met Jesus. He was considered one of the most knowledgeable men in the village on the meaning of Jesus 'life and message.

Jairus with his fifteen-year-old walking stick firmly in hand, taking a deep breath. His wife knew that when he had his old friend in hand, he was ready to face the people. He just couldn't speak without something in his hands. For all his sixty-two years it seemed his hands had to stay busy. With the walking stick in hand he had focus and steady nerves.

So it was, every week the people came the day after the Sabbath. Dozens of people, sometimes hundreds, made the trip to Jairus 'home in Capernaum to hear him speak for a few minutes. Through the years some had come over a hundred times, often bringing their friends. Many brought food and drink for the day. Today, the majority of them were there for the first time and they were about to hear a message that no one had ever heard, except in vague rumors. It was a message Jairus wasn't supposed to tell, a personal story—a message straight from Jesus Himself.

It was time to begin.

Jairus stepped out onto the portico and sang the traditional greeting, just as he had done so many times before:

"shema Yisroel adonaii elohanu, adonaii echod." *Meaning, 'Hear O Israel: The LORD our God is one LORD.'*

This traditional Jewish call to faith had been uttered for hundreds of years. The people settled down, he took a deep breath, and continued, "The greatest commandment is this: Thou shall love the LORD your God with all your heart, with all your mind, with all your soul, and with all your strength. And, the second is like to it: 'Love your neighbor as yourself.'"

With outstretched arms he summoned all to gather near, saying, "Greetings, my friends, in the name of Jesus of Nazareth, the true Messiah and the Christ. It's good to see so many old friends and I see many new faces, too.

"My name is Ya'ir, though people from foreign lands call me Jairus. For many years I have been spreading the message of the true Son of the living God. When Jesus walked among, us we didn't know His message was for all mankind, not just the Jews. When He was with us, we did not know who He was.

"Today, I want to talk about His messiah-ship. For many years we had waited for a messiah to deliver us from the Egyptians, Philistines, the Assyrians, and now the Romans. A messiah did come, but we didn't recognize Him.

"Jesus was who we needed, but not what we expected. He did not free us from the Romans. He was not a military leader who would destroy our earthly oppressors. He freed us from our fears, our sins, and bondage to the law.

"You may ask, 'What bondage? We need The Law of Moses. 'Well, I'll tell you. It was a good law, a just law, but it was written for a different people at a different time. Jesus, God's true Son, came to free us from the bondage of the law and now He has given us a new covenant, connecting us directly to the Father through Him. He has opened a way for all of us to have direct communion with God, just like Adam, Noah, and Father Abraham."

Jairus stopped for a moment and looked at his audience. Something was different; this audience was quieter than usual. More than that, their clothes were different. They had brought different food and drink. They were from other lands, perhaps far away.

Has my reputation traveled that far? Jairus thought. *No, not my reputation, but the Lord's Word has finally begun to spread to other regions. What a glorious time.*

Instantly, Jairus knew who they were and, acknowledging their presence, he continued, "I see we have many Greeks and Romans with us today. Are you followers of Jesus?"

People nodded and indicated they already believed and seemed anxious for more. "I'm honored to have you here.

"Gentile believers, praise to God on high!" Jairus said just a little under his breath.

"I've heard of the travels of The Great Rabbi's companions, but I had no idea so many people from so far away had been touched."

He gazed off in the distance. His mind was tightly focused, like he was searching for a day in his past. He was staring at a memory from long ago. Should he reveal what happened in those days? He was told to keep silent, but surely now the story can be told. He makes up his mind and continues.

"Since most of you are already believers in Jesus as the Christ, let me tell you a story that no one knows. It is a personal story of what Jesus did for me—*for ME!*" as he thumped his chest.

"Jesus Himself told me not to tell anyone, but I'm certain He intended for this story to be told someday to glorify the Father and Him. Today will be that day, and you are the first to hear the story of the day I found the Master, or maybe the Master found me. No matter, it was the day that changed my family forever."

Early Marriage

Jairus was nervous. After all, Jesus told him to keep silent, but everything Jesus did was for a larger purpose so by now it must be His will. Nearly twenty years had passed. He took a deep breath and started, "To understand the real point of the story, you must understand the beginning. This story starts when I was a young man.

"I had become an important synagogue official here in Capernaum. The synagogue was my responsibility; I made sure it was clean, in good repair, the floors were swept, the scrolls were well kept, rabbis were trained, and more. I had money, a house, a servant, and a position in the community. In other words, I was an important man in the religious and social life of Capernaum. I was a PERSON!"

He started overacting like a puffed up, overly proud, comical man. The reason Jairus was such a great storyteller was because he drew his audience into the story and kept their attention and he didn't mind making fun of himself.

"My new bride was seventeen when we met on our wedding day. I was twenty-seven. She was scared and I was so—well—I was, er… perhaps I was a little scared, too. Actually, I should tell you the truth, I was more scared than she was," he said with a big grin and a laugh.

Then, with a faux whisper and a wink to the house, he said, "And, sometimes I still am." A ripple of laughter goes through the crowd; he has their attention.

"As we grew to like each other and settle into our life, we worked to make a family. She kept a good Jewish house and after a short while, she told me I was going to be a father. Me, a papa. I would have a son and name him Levi. He would complete our love and we'd be a real family.

"I had great plans for little Levi. I would take him for long walks in the wilderness, teach him to live off the land, and to hunt and fish. I would teach him to read scripture and prepare the synagogue for services. Maybe he would follow in my footsteps. Then, in a few years, he would give me a grandson. Yes, I was to be a papa and then a grandpapa. My life's road ahead was set. After all, a man in my position *should* have a son, maybe even two or three or four."

Baby's Arrival

"The day came and Levi was ready to be born. He announced his arrival in the middle of the night. My wife sent me to get help. The midwives came and made me wait outside. I was so excited I was about to burst. I was going to be a papa! I gathered my closest friends to share the joy and to steady me just a little. We even toasted the baby's arrival a few times. Maybe we toasted a few too many times," he said with a winking laugh.

"The moment came, the midwife brought out a beautiful little bundle, and I finally was to meet my... *daughter*? Levi was a girl. My son was a girl?

"My disappointment lasted all of a heartbeat. She was the most beautiful little person I had ever seen. She had little fingers, and little toes, a little nose, and a little... well, you know what I mean."

He chuckled and said, "I had a daughter for one minute and I was already becoming a poet."

Jairus stopped for a moment and looked out over his new friends and wondered whether they were bored. He decided to make the story personal for them, too. Putting both hands on his staff and leaning forward as if the stick were a third leg, he asked, "I have a question for the men. How many of you have a daughter?"

A few of the men raised their hands or nodded in agreement, while a few were puzzled. They did not understand why he was asking. They didn't come all this way to hear an old man talk about his daughter.

Jairus continued, "Then you know the power this bundle of joy had over me. There's nothing quite so special as a daughter. She makes a home in your heart and she moves in and fills you with love and joy and such warmth of spirit. I found that I wasn't prepared for the power she would have over me. And, I was overjoyed to no end.

"Now, I have a question for the women: How many of you are daughters?" A laugh went through the crowd; actually, there weren't many women in attendance, but they responded and Jairus knew his new friends were listening.

"Did you build a home in your papa's heart? I'm sure you did." Saying this, Jairus was suddenly filled with love for his wife and daughter. They were his life and he was theirs. His eyes began misting over as he remembered all that happened so long ago. He swallowed hard and continued. "I don't know if my wife built a home in her papa's heart, but she lives in my heart, right next to my daughter."

Daughter's Childhood

"My daughter blessed my wife and me in ways we couldn't imagine. When she was a baby I loved spending time with her. I held her and fed her, and she caused me to love more than I could imagine. She made the little home in my heart grow warmer and brighter every day.

"The entire village knew her and of my love for her. I didn't care how it looked to others. When she and I walked in the wilderness I would teach her to hunt and fish. She appreciated the wilderness forests and rivers. My wife taught her how to keep a lawful house and I even taught her some woodworking.

"And, in spite of the Temple laws, I even taught her how to read. On her twelfth birthday she read a bit of the Scripture to us, that day my heart was ready to burst. I knew I was the proudest and most adoring papa in the region. My little girl meant the world to me. She had me wrapped around her little finger, exactly where I wanted to be." Another wink and a grin.

Her Illness

"One day, not long after she turned twelve, she was slow to rise and didn't eat much and drank little. She seemed tired and didn't want to go outside with her friends. We brought a physician to her, but he found no problem. In fact, he said that she was fine, just tired. But we knew it was more than that. Over the next few days she became weaker.

"One of the rabbis at the synagogue suggested we find a spiritual healer. This was considered a radical thing, especially for someone like me, but it was my daughter. By now she couldn't get out of bed. We found a healer and he came and recited chants over her and rubbed spices and herbs on her skin.

"Then, he picked her up out of the bed and lay her in my arms. He told me to hold her and walk around her bed three times while he continued praying and burning incense. To be honest, I felt silly, but what else could I do? And, the incense just made her coughing worse. These types of chants and incantations were against Temple Code, but she seemed near death and I was willing to do anything.

"After a while he said it was sin in *my* past that was causing her illness and I needed to purge it with certain rituals. He told me I had to make a blood offering, but not in the Temple where it was the usual way. I had never heard of a blood offering being performed in a home like mine, but I was ready to try anything. These were strange rituals to be sure. I had worked in the synagogue all my life and I had never heard of things like these, but my daughter was sick. The little home in my heart was growing cold. If it were my fault, I would try anything for her sake and do what the healer said.

"The healer told me what I needed to do. We needed to purchase a lamb without blemish, a pair of doves, and a small goat. Immediately my trusted servant and I went to the village. We split up; I went one way and he went another. It was not difficult to find the animals.

"When we returned to my house, we dug three small trenches and spilled the blood of each animal in a trench. This was difficult for me. I had never sacrificed any animal like this, at least not personally. I was never so grateful to have a servant with me than on that day. He knew exactly how to proceed. After the sacrifice I busied myself cleaning up the area and burying the carcasses. My mind was a whirl. It was difficult to focus on matters at hand. My daughter was my only concern.... And, how did my man know so much about what I needed? I thought I knew all about him.

"The healer had said that we must finish before sundown and we were just in time. I was told to sit and pray and ponder for the night. If my sins were forgiven, my daughter would be healed by morning. Hope began to fill my breast again but I dared not hope too much. Was our sacrifice enough? My good servant sat with me. He had become more than a servant—he had become a friend and an advisor.

"While we sat, he told me about a man, a rabbi, whom all of Capernaum was talking about. There were stories of Him casting out demons and healing a paralytic. 'Perhaps,' he said, 'maybe this was a true man of God.' I decided if the blood in the trenches failed, I would seek him out in the morning if there was time. Just thinking about what might happen to my little girl made the little home in my heart grow colder.

"The night was cold, so cold, and my heart was beginning to break. In spite of the urgency of the moment and our fears, we fell asleep. Not the restful sleep of the content, but a chaotic, choking sleep of the lost. I felt like I was Jacob wrestling with God all night. But, it wasn't God I was wrestling with, it was with the evil one, and I seemed to be losing.

"At sunrise we hurried into the house to see if the healing had begun. My wife hadn't slept and was at my daughter's side. One look at my wife told me what I needed to do next. My daughter's breathing was slow and labored; she was growing cold and wouldn't open her eyes. Her skin was grey, like dry sand, and it was obvious that her life was slipping away. I was helpless to do anything about it."

His voice began to crack as Jairus recalled the pain and fears he had felt so long ago. "My daughter was dying before my eyes. My world, my little heart-home, was crumbling. I was in such despair, I did not know what to do. There was no hope.

"When I told my wife what the servant had said about the new rabbi, she couldn't push me through the door fast enough.

"'Go, go 'was all she said. Sending me away to find Jesus. Then, she fell back into her grief. I told my servant to stay behind to comfort and assist my wife.

"I hurried off to the village center. My heart, which had always beat in tempo with my daughter's, was heavy and slow, my feet and legs were like stones. Could I find him? Would there be enough time? Was He even in Capernaum today?"

Finding and Returning with Jesus

Jairus slowed his story a little. He looked out over the crowd and saw he was having an unexpected effect. Tears were in their eyes and then he realized he was crying, too. All the memories and feelings from that day so long ago had come flooding over him like a torrent. Telling his story for the first time in public was taking its toll. He found himself leaning heavily on his stick. He regained his composure and continued.

"I was barely into the central village when I saw a crowd of people gathered around one man. *That must be him*, I thought. I moved faster, as fast as I could, but my legs would not obey me. They were too slow. I reached the edge of the crowd out of breath and with outstretched arms. Pushing and shoving my way to the middle I fell exhausted at Jesus 'feet.

"To this day I'm not sure if I was honoring Him or just fell down, too tired to stand upright.

"I do remember thinking, *This is the moment. What do I say? Do I beg, do I plead, or do I demand? Am I worthy? All these people around us know me, they know what I do. They know what I am. I should be embarrassed, but I'm not, I'm desperate and I don't care what anyone thinks.* All these thoughts flooded through me in the blink of an eye.

"There I was, at His feet. I looked up into Jesus 'eyes and knew exactly what I had to say. Without any effort at all, the words just came out of me. They weren't even my words.

"I said something like... 'Lord, my daughter is near death. I know you have the power to heal. She's fighting for every breath. Please, I beseech you, come to my house and save her. I know you can.'"

Jairus took a breath and swallowed hard. He wasn't just telling a story, he was reliving the whole episode. He continued, "I knew He could. How did I know? I don't know but I did. Somehow I knew He could help. He offered to go with me and relief began to fill my soul.

"I got to my feet with some effort, but just as we turned to leave, He stopped and asked, 'Who touched me?'"

That Was My Miracle

"Who touched me?" Jairus remembers the moment: "There were dozens, perhaps hundreds, of people around Him and He asked who touched Him? It didn't make sense; he was being touched by practically every person there. Even his disciples said, 'Master, everyone is touching you.'

"Then, like as one, the crowd began to cleave away from Him. They watched in near silence as Jesus faced a familiar woman."

Jairus remembers his anger. "Wait! I knew her, we all knew her! She was a wretched thing! She's nothing! She smelled bad. Everyone in the village avoided any contact with her. We all knew she was unclean and not allowed in the synagogue. A woman that vile is not worthy of this teacher's time. Why is she bothering Him? She's a mess and my daughter is clean and pure, and dying.

"I watched in horror as she fell down at Jesus 'feet and confessed all. My heart was pounding so hard I couldn't hear what she said. But, the amazing thing is that before his disciples could remove her, Jesus knelt down, touched her face, and said, '*Daughter, thy faith hath made thee whole, go in peace, and be whole of thy plague.* 'In that moment it seemed like they were the only two people in the whole world. For a moment I even forgot about my mission.

"She changed in an instant; we could see it in her face and eyes. She was suddenly at peace and I became angry! He healed her! How could He? That was my miracle! My daughter is dying and He's wasting His time with this outcast. He tells her to go in peace and my daughter is dying. I have no peace, why should she? I was beginning to wonder if I placed my faith in the wrong man. I wanted to lash out, but at whom? I had an anger in my gut that was almost uncontrollable.

"'Wait, calm down,' some little voice in me said, telling me to stop and think. He called her 'daughter,' why did He call her daughter? She's obviously not his daughter. A small piece of me understood. Maybe all daughters are worthy of being healed. I never thought of her as someone's daughter, just an undesirable village nuisance. Does she have a papa? Did her papa love her like I loved my daughter? Did she make a home in his heart, too?

"Or, was He calling her 'daughter 'as if she were His own daughter? Maybe He knows her father has nothing to do with her now and He's wishing to be a substitute. Really, who is this man?

"Just then I saw my servant running toward me, his face telling me what I did not want to hear. He said, 'There's no reason to bother the teacher anymore, your daughter is dead.'" He said it plainly, without emotion or apology. Except, I saw his eyes misting. He wasn't cold, he was trying to hold his emotions in check.

"Dead, how could that be? If this woman hadn't sneaked into the crowd or if Jesus hadn't lingered so long, we might have made it to my house in time. It's over, no more hope, no more little home of love and warmth in my heart. I was dead inside, just like my daughter.

"Before I could even begin to mourn, Jesus touched my shoulder and looked me in the eye, and said, 'Don't be afraid but believe. 'I started breathing again and felt a small wave of relief. He seemed confident and that helped.

"His words offered a little comfort, and I was confused. I tried to believe, I think I believed. No matter, I still needed to rush Him to my house. Jesus turned to go with me and brought three of his disciples, sending the rest of the crowd away. He seemed confident, but I was still unsure.

"As we approached the house we could hear the mourners. They were cousins and neighbors of mine and they knew my little girl had died. It had been less than an hour since my servant told me the bad news. They had no business being there. This was my grief. It seemed everyone knew my daughter had died except Jesus Himself, and now, strangely, I was beginning to trust in His calm assurances and believe that He could restore her. I believed in Him, and the little home in my heart was already getting a bit warmer and brighter. It seemed to take forever to get to my house."

The Miracle

"When we arrived, Jesus turned to the mourners and asked, 'Why do you weep and wail? The child isn't dead, she's only sleeping. 'They ridiculed Him, so he sent them away with the manner of a man who was not to be denied.

"He took His three followers and me into the house. My wife was sobbing in the corner. She couldn't look on my daughter's body. I went to her side as we watched Jesus pass straight to our daughter.

"Then it happened. It didn't seem like enough. It happened with a word.

"Jesus walked straight to my daughter's bed and with a touch and a word He restored my daughter's life. Just a touch, just a word, there were no strange rituals. He didn't spend hours chanting, or blaming my sin, He didn't really examine her, He just touched her hand and said, 'talitha cumi,' meaning in our tongue, 'little girl arise.' That's all, just a simple gesture and speaking 'little girl arise' and my daughter got up from her bed and walked straight over to us.

"Saying it out loud doesn't seem to give the miracle

enough power. A simple act from one man accomplished the greatest thing I had ever seen.

"We had no time to think or react. My little girl was dead a moment ago and now she lives and standing at our side. You can guess what was happening to the home in my heart now.

"My wife cried for joy as my daughter stood with us. I didn't know what to say or think. Had she really been dead? Maybe Jesus shook her out of her sleep. No, that can't be. He barely touched her hand. He must have used the same power on that woman. But Jesus said that other woman's faith had healed her. Was my faith really that strong? But I didn't have faith, not like that woman on the streets. Perhaps I had a little hope, but no real faith. It was my wife who sent me to find the teacher. Perhaps it was her faith. I never really asked, it didn't matter, not then.

"My miracle was so quick and over with in a moment. It didn't seem like enough, but there was my little girl, alive and standing right next to us. Her living face couldn't be questioned.

"Jesus left us with two commands. He told us to feed her because she was still ashen and weak. And—strangely—**not to tell anyone what had happened**. Then He and His followers were gone. They just left without another word. We were so overjoyed to have our daughter back, we barely noticed they had left us. It's hard to admit now but my wife and I were sobbing so hard with joy we didn't know we were alone. My daughter seemed to be wondering what all the fuss was about. We all started laughing out loud and holding each other like never before."

Jairus looked a little wistful for a moment as he remembered the three men. "Peter, James, and John. I'm not sure what happened to James, but Peter and John have gone on to be strong voices for the new Messiah. I have visited with them from time to time over the last ten years.

"Yes, I said, 'Messiah.' I knew then and I know now that Jesus was, rather *is*, our Messiah."

Aftermath

"I didn't understand. Why couldn't we tell anyone? I wanted to shout the news from the top of the Temple but we kept it to ourselves as we were told. It didn't matter. Everyone would know what happened. They all knew she had died, yet there she was playing with friends, going to synagogue services and the market. It was only later I realized He didn't want to call attention to Himself just yet. We needed to keep silent for His ministry to unfold.

"Some people talked openly and some whispered, but no one outside my house really knew what Jesus did for ME! His deeds and His Word cannot be stifled. The home in my heart was filled again with love, love for my wife and daughter, love for The Lord and His message. That's why I come out here every week and proclaim His Kingdom and message of redemption. Now, he has a home in my heart right next to my daughter's.

"Maybe my faith that day wasn't enough to heal my daughter, but His love was. I followed Jesus 'ministry from that day forward.

"Over time I have seen the number of His followers grow steadily. John convinced me beyond a doubt that Jesus walked away from his tomb. I am convinced, after watching Him raise my dead daughter and learning He himself arose from the grave, that He and His message must be heard and spread to all the world. He is truly God's own Son.

"Resurrected lives, that's the Jesus touch. He touched my daughter; it was like she was born again to a resurrected life. He did it at least twice more, once to a widow's son, and again to His friend Lazarus, not to mention the hundreds of lives His message has changed. My life, my wife's life and many of you, my friends, are all changed by knowing Him and His teachings. We have all been brought into new and resurrected lives.

"Now, as I come to a close, you have heard a different type of message than I've told in the past. This was the first time this story was spoken in public. I hope you go out and tell others. Tell them what Jesus did for me and my daughter, and tell them your stories, too. Tell them what Jesus did for you and what He did for all of us. Surely as He raised my daughter, He can lead us all to the Father. Jesus gave His life as payment for our sins. Yes, my sins are finally forgiven, but it wasn't the blood of three animals, it was the blood of the Son. All He asks of us is that we believe in Him and we can have everlasting life.

"I asked for my daughter's life and He provided. If you ask to have your sin forgiven, He will. You will see your life change. Contentment and peace will fill you like living water to cleanse your soul."

Jairus looked out over the crowd one more time, anticipating questions and discussion. He sensed enough had been said.

"Now, my new friends, I will bid you good day. I will close with a short prayer for your safe journey home."

Then, another thought struck him. "Oh, a bit more news. My daughter has given me another blessing. She bore me a grandson. She named him Levi. And remember that other woman He healed? She and my daughter have the Lord's healing love in common. They've become friends and we often welcome her into our home. Now I have so much warmth and love, so many little homes filling my heart and my life. I've never known love like this!"

Jairus said a short prayer for safe travel and dismissed his new friends. As he watched them depart, a warm glow filled his chest and he chuckled to himself.

Little homes in hearts. Where did that come from? What a funny thing to say, he thought, *but true, so true. Thank you, Lord,* aloud to himself as he turned and looked up to the heavens, *for everything.*

About Atmosphere Press

Atmosphere Press is an independent, full-service publisher for excellent books in all genres and for all audiences. Learn more about what we do at atmospherepress.com.

We encourage you to check out some of Atmosphere's latest releases, which are available at Amazon.com and via order from your local bookstore:

Great Spirit of Yosemite: The Story of Chief Tenaya, nonfiction by Paul Edmondson

My Cemetery Friends: A Garden of Encounters at Mount Saint Mary in Queens, New York, nonfiction and poetry by Vincent J. Tomeo

Change in 4D, nonfiction by Wendy Wickham

Disruption Games: How to Thrive on Serial Failure, nonfiction by Trond Undheim

Eyeless Mind, nonfiction by Stephanie Duesing

A Blameless Walk, nonfiction by Charles Hopkins

The Horror of 1888, nonfiction by Betty Plombon

White Snake Diary, nonfiction by Jane P. Perry

From Rags to Rags, essays by Ellie Guzman

Giving Up the Ghost, essays by Tina Cabrera

Family Legends, Family Lies, nonfiction by Wendy Hoke

About the Author

Rev. Dr. Rodney E. Cleaves grew up in South Portland, Maine, and at an early age developed a love of theatre, music, and art. However, because of the responsibilities of a growing family he opted for a "safe" career in technology, and was an engineer and computer scientist. 

Recently retired from his day job, he is an avid photographer, and now writer. He and his wife Elaine are also loving parents to six grown (or growing) children and they count thirty-nine grandchildren. Foster parents to nearly 500 more kids, when asked why so many, they reply, "It's an investment in the future."

He also wrote this little bio in third person so it wouldn't sound so selfish.